Black Beauty

With a discussion of
KINDNESS

Cover illustration by
Jael

www.readingchallenge.com

a division of
Learning Challenge, Inc.
569 Boylston Street
Boston, MA 02116

Manufactured in the United States of America
0203-1CG

Library of Congress Cataloging-in-Publication Data

Wood, Leigh Hope.
Black Beauty : and a discussion of kindness / by Anna Sewell ; adapted by Leigh Hope Wood ;
illustrated by Richard Martin.
p. cm. -- (Values in action illustrated classics)
Summary: A simplified, abridged version of Black Beauty's experiences with both good and bad masters in nineteenth-century
England, accompanied by a short biography of Anna Sewell and an essay focusing on the story's lessons of kindness.
ISBN 1-59203-028-9
1. Horses--Juvenile fiction. [1. Horses--Fiction. 2. Kindness--Fiction.] I. Martin, Richard, ill. II. Sewell, Anna, 1820-1878.
Black Beauty. III. Title. IV. Series.
PZ10.3.W773Bl 2003
[Fic]--dc21   2002156663

VALUES IN ACTION ™
Illustrated Classics

Black Beauty

by
Anna Sewell

With a discussion of
KINDNESS

Adapted by
Leigh Hope Wood

Illustrated by
Richard Martin

Dear Parents and Educators:

Reading Challenge™ is pleased to introduce a new Literacy and Character Education program—**Values in Action™ Illustrated Classics.**

These adapted, timeless tales are perfect for classroom study, homeschooling, and supplemental reading. The stories foster an appreciation of important values that form the basis of sound character education. In addition, each book contains a value-discussion section, a glossary/pronunciation guide, and a short biography of the author.

A full list of **Values in Action Illustrated Classics** available through Reading Challenge can be found at the back of each book.

"Open a book . . . and the world opens to you."

The Editors
Reading Challenge

A division of Learning Challenge, Inc.
www.learningchallenge.com

Kindness in Action

How *Black Beauty* Illustrates the Value of Kindness

Black Beauty is the story of a horse living in England in the 1800s. As an animal, Black Beauty is at the mercy of humans. They have all the power. When Black Beauty is a colt, his mother tells him to always be kind and gentle and he will be treated kindly and gently in return. As it turns out, this is not always true.

Kindness, to both people and animals, is very important. There are many ways to be kind. One type of kindness is just being nice to other people. For example, you say "Excuse me" when you bump into someone. Or you remember your friend's birthday. Another way of being kind is to go out of your way to do things that make other people happy. For example, you surprise your best friend with a cupcake, because you know she loves them. A third type of kindness is seeking out sad or needy people and trying to help them. Volunteering to help the poor is an example of this type of kindness.

The true test of kindness comes when you are dealing with a person, or animal, who is weaker than you. Why? It is easy to be kind to someone who has power over you or can do something for you. Think about it: When you want your mother or father to buy you something, you find it pretty easy to be nice, right? But what about when someone wants something from you? Are you kind when you have the power?

As an animal, Black Beauty is at the mercy of the humans around him. This book shows what happens when people lose sight of kindness and behave in cruel ways. It also reminds us how important it is to show true kindness to animals as well as humans.

Contents

PART ONE

PART THREE

PART FOUR

Part

1

Chapter

1

My First Home

Looking back, to when I was a very young colt, I think of the beautiful meadow where I lived. It had a clear pond and shady trees. From it I could see a plowed field to one side and my master's house on the other side. At the top were fir trees, and at the bottom there was a brook with a steep bank.

In those early days, I lived on my mother's milk and always stayed by her side. But as soon as I was old enough to eat grass, she had to go to work during the day. I played in the meadow with the other colts, who were older and very big. Sometimes we played very rough—galloping, kicking, and biting. When my mother saw us one day, she called me over.

"Your friends are very good colts," she said, "but they have not learned manners. I don't think you have ever seen me bite. Lift your feet up when you trot and never bite or kick. I want you to grow up gentle and never learn bad ways."

I always tried to remember her advice, because I knew my mother was wise. Our master certainly favored her. My mother's name was Duchess, but he called her Pet. Whenever she saw the master at the gate, she would trot over. He would then pat her and say, "Well, old Pet, and how is your little Smoky?" I was a dull black, so that was the name he called me by.

Our master was kind, and we liked him. But there was also a young plowboy named Dick, who sometimes came to our meadow to pick berries. He had fun throwing stones and sticks at us

Most of the time he missed hitting us because we galloped off. But when he did get us, it hurt very much.

One day, when Dick was playing this little game, our master was in another field and saw him. He came running over the hedge and caught Dick by the arm.

"You're a bad boy to chase the colts! But you won't get the chance to do it anymore. Take your pay and go home. I don't need you here."

Old Daniel, the man who looked after all of us, was as gentle as our master. So, when Dick left, we were very well off.

Chapter

② My Training

As I grew, my coat became soft and bright black in color. I had one white foot and a white star on my forehead, and I was said to be handsome and strong.

My master would not sell me until I was at least four years old. He said that young boys should not work until they were men, and colts should not work until they were fully grown horses.

When I was four, a man called Squire Gordon came to take a look at me. He said that once I had been broken in, I would do very well. My master said

he would break me in himself, because he did not want me to be frightened or hurt.

To break in a horse means to teach him or her to wear a saddle and bridle. A horse must also learn how to pull a cart and know when the master wants to go fast or slow. A horse must always do what the master wants, even if the horse is tired or hungry. So you can easily see that getting broken in is a difficult thing to go through.

I was used to wearing a halter and

being led around in the field, but I was not used to the bit and bridle. A bit is a thick piece of cold steel that goes between your teeth and over your tongue. The ends come out at the corners of your mouth and connect to the straps of the bridle.

My master gave me some oats and gently put the bridle over my head and the bit in my mouth. I didn't like it at all, but I knew my mother and the other horses wore one. So, with my master's pats and kind words, as well as the oats, I got used to wearing my bit and bridle.

Next, I learned to wear the saddle

and rode my master around the meadow. Then came the iron shoes. This was done by a blacksmith. He took a piece of iron the shape of my foot and nailed one to each hoof. It didn't hurt at all. The shoes felt heavy at first, but in time I got used to them.

Having come so far, I then learned to wear a harness and many other things. I had to get used to having a stiff heavy collar on my neck and a bridle with blinkers on my eyes. Blinkers are pieces of leather that sit on the side of your face next to your eyes. Wearing them, I could not see to either side, but only straight ahead. There was also a small saddle with a strap that went right under my tail. This was the crupper. I didn't like it at all, but I finally got used to it and all the other things I had to wear.

Another part of my training was to spend two weeks in a meadow next to railroad tracks. There, I heard and saw a train for the first time. I was very frightened and took off for the other side

of the field. In time, though, I saw how the cows went on eating without noticing the train. So I, too, learned to ignore it. Since then, I have seen many horses throw their riders or run at the sight of a train. Thanks to my master, I am as fearless at a railway station as I am in my own stable.

My master often drove me in a double harness with my mother. She was steady and could teach me better than a strange horse could. She told me to behave well and I would be treated kindly. She also told me about people.

"Some are kind like your master, but some are cruel or foolish," she warned. "These people shouldn't have a horse or dog. I can only hope that you will fall into good hands, my dear."

Chapter

3

Birtwick Park

In early May, a man came from Squire Gordon's, and my master said good-bye to me. I put my nose into his hand, and he patted me kindly. Then I left my first home for a place called Birtwick Park, where I lived for several years.

The Park lay outside the village of Birtwick. The entrance was a large iron gate. A smooth road, lined by large old trees, led to the house and gardens. There was also a place for many horses and carriages.

I was put into a "loose" box, where I was not tied up but left to do as I wished. The other stalls in my stable were common stalls. They were nice but not nearly so large as the loose box. I was never in as good a home as that. It was clean and airy.

The groom who put me in my box gave me some oats and patted me. He spoke kindly to me and then went away. I looked around and saw in the next stall a little fat gray pony with a thick mane and tail.

"How do you do?" I said. "What is your name?"

"My name is Merrylegs," he said. "I carry the young ladies on my back, and sometimes I take our mistress out. They think a great deal of me, and so does James. Are you going to live next door to me in the box?"

"Yes," I answered.

"Well, then. I hope you are good-tempered. I do not like anyone next door who bites," he said.

Another horse looked over from a stall beyond. It was a tall chestnut mare. Her ears were laid back, and her eyes looked ill-tempered. She looked across at me.

"So it is you who have pushed me out of my box," she said. "It is a very strange thing for a colt like you to turn a lady out of her home."

"I beg your pardon," I said. "I turned no one out. The young man who brought me was the one who put me here. I had nothing to do with it.

Besides, I am not a colt but a grown-up horse, and I wish to live in peace."

"Well," she said, "we shall see. Of course, I do not wish to have words with a young thing like you."

Nothing else was said, and in the afternoon, when the mare went out, Merrylegs told me all about her.

"Ginger has a bad habit of biting and snapping. That is why they call her Ginger. One day, when she was in the loose box, she bit James on the arm and made it bleed. Miss Flora and Miss Jessie, who are very fond of me, were afraid to come into the stable. They used to bring me nice things to eat, an apple or a carrot. I miss them. I hope they will now come again, if you don't bite or snap."

"I have never bitten anything but grass, hay, and corn," I said.

"Well, it is a bad habit with Ginger. She says no one was ever kind to her, and why shouldn't she bite. If all she says is true, she was treated very badly before she came here. But John does all he can to please her, and James does all he can, and our master never uses a whip if a horse acts right. I am twelve years old, and I can tell you there is no better place for a horse than this. John is the best groom and James is a kind boy. So, it is all Ginger's fault that she did not stay in that box."

Chapter

4

A Fair Start

The name of the coachman was John Manly. He had a wife and a little child. They lived in a cottage very near the stables. One morning, on my master's instructions, John took me out for a ride. We rode slowly at first, then trotted, cantered, and finally galloped.

When we came back to the Park, we met the Squire and Mrs. Gordon walking. John jumped off and began to talk to them.

"Well, John, how does he go?" asked the Squire.

"First-rate, sir," answered John. "He is as fast and quick as a deer and has a fine spirit, too. Yet he is easily guided by the rein."

"That's good," said the Squire. "I will try him myself tomorrow."

The next day, my master took me out. I found he was a very good rider and thoughtful of his horse. When we came home, the lady was at the door.

"Well, my dear," she said, "how do you like him?"

"He is exactly what John said," he replied. "What shall we call him?"

"He is really quite a beauty, and he has such a sweet face," she said thoughtfully. "What do you say to calling him Black Beauty?"

"Yes! I think that's a fine name," he answered. "If you like, that shall be his name."

When John took me back to the stable, he told James about my name. John seemed very proud of me. He brushed me until I was glossy and talked to me all the time. James Howard, the stable boy, was just as gentle.

I grew very fond of John and James, and I became very good friends with Merrylegs. I got along with Ginger, who often shared the work with me in pulling the carriage. There were also two horses named Justice and Sir Oliver, who stood in another stable. Justice and I talked whenever we got the chance.

I was very happy in my new place, but I missed my freedom. Now, week after week, month after month, and probably year after year, I would have to stand up in a stable night and day waiting until I was wanted. Then I would have to be steady and quiet, wearing straps here and there, a bit in my mouth, and blinkers over my eyes.

I knew this was the way it had to be, but I had so much spirit that I wanted to

fling back my head and gallop away at full speed. Sometimes I must have shaken John up with my jumping, dancing, and prancing around. But he was always good and patient.

"Steady, steady, my boy," he would say. "We'll soon have a good ride."

He would take me out for a few miles of trotting and bring me back fresh and ready. Spirited horses are often called skittish when really they are only full of play. They need exercise, but some grooms will punish them instead.

Chapter

5

Ginger

One day, Ginger and I stood alone in the shade and talked for awhile. She asked about my upbringing and breaking in, and I told her all about it.

"Well," she said, "if I had experienced what you have, I might have had as good a temper as you. Now, I don't think I ever shall."

"Why not?" I asked.

"I've had so many people be cruel to me," she said. "I was taken from my mother when I was very young and put with a lot of other colts. Our master never gave us kind words, and young boys threw rocks at us. When it came time for my breaking in, some men came by and surrounded me and forced the bit into my mouth. One dragged me by the halter, and another followed behind whipping me. I kicked and pulled, but they kept whipping me.

"Then, later, my master's son came to the small dark stall where I was being kept. He wanted to break my spirits. If I did not do exactly as he wanted, he would run me around the training field until I was so tired that I could hardly stand.

"One day, he worked me so hard that I lay down. He came the very next morning and ran me around the track. When I began to grow tired, he whipped me. I couldn't stand it any longer. I kicked and reared, and finally I threw him from me and ran off.

"I stood in a field, hungry and thirsty, for a long time. Finally an old man came and talked gently to me. He led me to the stable and washed my wounds with fresh water. He came to see me often, and another trainer began to teach me. He was gentle, and I finally learned what was expected of me.

"So, that was my breaking in. And afterwards, I met up with one cruel man after another. I learned to bite and kick to defend myself. Of course, it is very different here, but who knows how long that will last?"

"Well," I said. "I think it would be a real shame if you were to bite or kick John or James."

"I don't mean to while they are good

to me," she said. "I did bite James pretty sharp, but he treated me kindly even so. I have never snapped at him since."

I felt very sorry for Ginger, and I found that, as the weeks went on, she grew more gentle and cheerful under the care of James and John.

Chapter

6

Merrylegs

One day, Mr. Blomefield, the town clergyman, came to the house with his large family of boys and girls. Whenever they visited, there was plenty of work for Merrylegs, because the children loved to ride him.

On this day, James brought Merrylegs back into the stable after a long time out in the field.

"There, now," he said, as he put on Merrylegs's halter, "you better behave or we shall get into trouble."

"What did you do, Merrylegs?" I asked.

"I have been giving those children a lesson," he said. "They did not know when they had had enough of me, or when I had had enough of them. So, I just threw them off my back."

"You threw the children off!" I said, a little shocked.

"Actually, it was one of the boys. After more than two hours of the other children riding me, he decided he wanted his turn. He cut a whip out of a hazel stick and hit me with it. I tried to warn

him by stopping very suddenly two or three times, but he kept hitting me. So, I just rose up and let him slip off."

"If I had been you," said Ginger, "I would have given him a good kick."

"No, I wouldn't do that," Merrylegs replied. "I wouldn't want to make James ashamed of me. Besides, my master trusts me. If I took to kicking, where would I be? I would be sold off to a place where no one cared for me. I don't want that. I love our people. They have always been kind to me."

Chapter

7

A Talk in the Garden

Ginger and I were both more race horse than large carriage horse. We were just as good for riding as for driving. Our greatest pleasure was when we were saddled for a riding party. The master rode on Ginger, the mistress on me, and the young ladies on Sir Oliver and Merrylegs.

I had often wondered why Sir Oliver had such a short tail. On one of our holidays, when we were let loose in the orchard, I asked him about it.

"It was a cruel act!" he exclaimed. "I was very young and was taken to a place and tied up so that I couldn't move. Then they came and cut my tail. They cut right through the flesh."

"How awful!" I said.

"It was awful! It was not only painful, but outrageous. My dignity was greatly injured when they took my tail away. Besides, I needed my tail. I can't tell you how aggravating it is to have flies land on you, and you're not able to brush them off. Thank heaven people no longer cut tails off."

"Why did they do it at that time?" asked Ginger.

"For fashion!" exclaimed Sir Oliver. "Someone decided horses needed short tails to look good. Look what they do to dogs. They cut off their tails and pin back their ears to make them look cute."

"Ah! They are all so mean!" Ginger said excitedly.

"Well," I said. "Can anyone tell me about the use of blinkers?"

"They are supposed to keep horses from getting frightened," replied Justice.

"I think blinkers are dangerous things, especially in the night," said Sir Oliver. "Many accidents might never have happened if horses had had full use of their eyes. Horses, after all, can see much better than people."

"I'll tell you a secret," said Merrylegs. "I believe John does not approve of blinkers. I heard him tell the master that it would be a good thing if colts were broken in without blinkers. So, let's cheer up and run to the other end of the orchard. The wind has blown down some apples."

We then made ourselves feel better by munching on some very sweet apples that lay scattered on the grass.

Chapter

8

A Stormy Day

Late in autumn one day, my master had to go on a long business journey, and John was to go with him. I was hitched to a cart, and we all set out.

It had rained a great deal, and after awhile the wind picked up. As we came to a low wooden toll bridge, we could see that the river was high. The man at the gate said the river was rising fast. We got over, but in some places the water was halfway up to my knees.

Once in town, we stayed a long time and didn't set out for home until late in the afternoon. Back on the road, the wind was blowing hard, and the great branches of the trees were swaying about like twigs. Suddenly, there was a groan and a crack. A great oak, torn up by its roots, came crashing down in our path.

"That was a close call," said my master. "What shall we do now?"

"Well, we can't drive over it or get around it," answered John. "We must go back to the crossway, about six miles back. It will make us late, but Black Beauty is still strong."

We turned around and headed

back. By the time we got to the toll bridge, the water was over the middle of it. John did not call me to a stop, but the moment my foot touched the bridge I knew something was wrong. I didn't dare go forward. John tapped me lightly with the whip, but I refused to go.

"There's something wrong, sir," said John, as he got down from the cart. He came forward to lead me, but I still wouldn't go.

Just then the man from the tollgate ran out of the house from the other side of the river and cried for us to halt.

"What's the matter?" shouted John.

"The bridge is broken in the middle," he yelled.

"Thank God for Black Beauty!" exclaimed my master.

John turned me around. The sun had set, and it was growing darker and darker. As we went along, my master and John talked about how animals had often saved people's lives.

At last we came to the Park gates safely. As we pulled up to the house, the mistress came out. She was very glad to see us, for she had been worried that we had had an accident. My master assured her that we were all right.

"We got here safely," he said, "but only because of our dear Black Beauty."

Chapter 9

James Howard

One morning early in December, John was leading me into my box after my exercise and James was coming in from the corn chamber, when the master walked in.

"Good morning, John," said my master. "I want to know if you have any complaints about James, here."

"No, sir," answered John. "He is the smartest, most pleasant and honest young fellow I've had in this stable. I trust his work."

"James," said my master, "I am very

glad to find that John has a high opinion of you. I have a letter from my brother-in-law. He needs a trustworthy fellow to become his coachman. I want to recommend you for the job. It would be a big step, so think it over and talk to your family. Let me know what you decide."

"Thank you, sir," said James, very excitedly.

Soon it was decided that James would take the job. In the meantime, while he was still at Birtwick Park, he got plenty of practice driving. Ginger and

I were hitched to the wagon, and James held the reins.

On one trip, we traveled about forty-six miles away, so that the master and mistress could visit some friends. The first day, James drove the carriage for thirty-two miles. He drove very carefully, keeping our feet on the smoothest part of the road. He put the brake on when going downhill and took it off going up.

When we arrived in the town where we were to spend the night, James led Ginger and me to a stable. Two men who worked there rubbed us down, and James left to get some rest.

Much later, I heard a horse being led in. As he was rubbed down for the night, a man sat by smoking a pipe and talking to the groom. After a while, the groom asked the young man to put out his pipe and throw some hay into the horses' rack, which the man did. Then the door was locked, and we were left for the night.

I don't know how long I slept, but I awoke feeling uneasy. The air was thick,

and I could hardly breathe. I could see very little but I could tell the other horses were restless. I trembled all over with fear.

At last I heard someone in the stable. It was the groom. He was untying the horses and trying to lead them out. He seemed very frightened, causing us to be even more frightened. We all refused to go with him. He finally gave up and left the stable.

There was a rushing sound overhead in the loft, and as it grew louder I could see red light flickering on the wall. Suddenly, I heard James's quiet and comforting voice.

"Come, my beauties," he said. "It is time to wake up and leave this place."

I was near the door, so he came to me first. He put his scarf over my eyes and talked to me gently, leading me out into the yard. There, he took the scarf from my eyes and left me with another man, then headed back into the burning stable. I whinnied when I saw him go.

The smoke was now pouring out of the stable door, but I kept watching it for James to come out. There was much confusion. People were shouting from every direction. Then I heard my master's voice.

"James Howard," he shouted. "James Howard!"

Finally, from the door of the stable, James appeared leading a horse. It was Ginger! She was coughing violently, and James was unable to speak.

"When you have caught your breath, lad," said my master, "we will get out of here as quickly as we can."

Soon, we were hurrying to the marketplace. My master found another hotel and went off to get the mistress. James put us to bed in another stable. We were glad to be safe, but we felt sad about those poor horses left in the burning stable.

Chapter 10

James Takes His Leave

The next day, we set out on our journey. The distance was shorter, so the traveling was a little easier. Just after sunset, we reached the house of my master's friend, and we were taken to a cozy stable.

There was a kind coachman there who, after hearing about the fire, had many kind things to say to James.

"Young man, it is clear that your horses know whom they can trust," he said. "It is the hardest thing in the world to get horses out of a stable when there is a fire or a flood. I salute you, young man!"

We stayed at this place for only a few days. Then, we returned to Birtwick Park. The journey home went well, and we were glad to be back in our stable.

John was just as glad to see us. He and James talked awhile. James asked who would be replacing him.

"Little Joe Green at the Lodge," replied John.

"Why, he's a child!" exclaimed James.

"He is fourteen and a half," said John. "He is small but quick and willing, and kindhearted, too. I know the master would like to give him a chance."

The next day we met Joe Green. He came to the stables to learn as much as he could before James left. He could sweep the stables and bring in the hay, but he was too short to groom Ginger and me.

James had to show Joe how to groom on Merrylegs, who complained about being cared for by a "child who

knew nothing." By the next week, though, Merrylegs confessed that Joe was learning well.

Finally, the day came for James to leave. He looked very unhappy. He said he would miss his friends and family as well as the horses he loved so much. But John cheered up James by reminding him that he would meet new friends and would make his family proud.

After James left, Merrylegs moped about for weeks. John had to take him out and let him gallop in the fields every morning. We were all sad to see James go. He had treated us all with a special kindness.

Chapter

11

Going for the Doctor

One night, a few days after James left, I was awakened by the stable bell ringing. Suddenly John came in, calling out to me.

"Wake up, Beauty," he said. "You must run better now than you ever have."

In no time he had the bridle over my head and saddle on my back. He then grabbed his coat and took me at a quick trot to the master's door. The Squire stood there with a lamp in his hand.

"Now, John," he said, "ride for your life, that is, for the mistress' life. Give this note to Doctor White. Then give Beauty a rest at the inn before returning."

"I will, sir," replied John.

He jumped on my back, and we rode fast. We rode past the gardener, who stood at the open gate. Then, leaving the Park with great speed, we went through the village to the tollgate. Soon we were on level road, and I galloped as fast as I could lay my feet to the ground.

After eight miles of hard running, we came to the town. As we drew up to Doctor White's place, John jumped off and began banging on the door. The doctor threw open his window and looked out.

"What do you want?" he cried.

"Mrs. Gordon is very ill, sir," replied John. "Master wants you to come at once. He thinks she will die if you cannot get there. Here is his note."

The doctor came down and took the note.

"This is terrible. On top of it, I've had my horse out all day, and he's tired. My son has been called out, too, tonight, and he has the other horse. Can I ride your horse?"

"He has galloped all the way here, but I think it will be all right," answered John. "Please do take care of him."

"I will," promised the doctor.

When Doctor White was ready, he came out of the house, carrying a riding whip.

"Sir, you won't be needing that," John said. "Black Beauty will go until he drops."

The doctor climbed on, and we set off in a hurry. He was heavier than John and not as good a rider, but we made it to the Park in good time. When we arrived at the door, Doctor White headed into the house. Then, I was led to the stable.

I was glad to get home. My legs were shaking, and my beautiful coat was wet all over. Joe rubbed my legs and my chest, but he thought I was too hot to be covered with my thick warm blanket. He gave me a cold pail of water, which I drank quickly, and some corn and hay. After all this, Joe thought he had done what he should, and he left the stable.

Soon I began to shake and tremble. My legs and body ached, and I would have loved to have my blanket. I longed for John to come home and take care of me, but I knew he had eight miles to walk. It would be a while, so I lay down in the straw.

When John finally arrived, I was moaning and in great pain. He stooped

Black Beauty

down and covered me with many blankets. He then gave me some hot porridge which I drank with great pleasure, but he seemed very upset.

"Stupid boy!" John said aloud. "Not only did he not cover you up, he probably gave you cold water as well."

John nursed me night and day. My master, too, came out to see me. I heard John tell him he had never seen a horse run so fast. It was as if, he said, I knew what was the matter. Of course, I had known.

"My poor Beauty," said my master. "You saved your mistress' life."

Chapter 12

Joe Green

For a very long time, John was angry with Joe. It was only after I got well that he could speak kindly to the young boy. Even though Joe had done what he thought was best, it had been bad for me. John felt that ignorance was no excuse for doing harm. However Joe was a kind boy and got the chance again to show his good character.

One day, when John was out with Justice in the luggage cart, the master sent orders for Joe to saddle me and take a note to a gentleman's house about three miles away. Joe rode carefully, and we delivered the note. We were quietly returning when we came to the brickfield.

There was a cart heavily loaded with bricks and stuck in the mud. The carter was shouting and whipping two horses, trying to get them to pull the cart out. The horses were working as hard as they could, but the cart was just too heavy.

"Hold on," Joe screamed. "I'll help you. Please don't whip the horses any more."

"Mind your own business, and I'll mind mine," said the carter.

Joe turned me around, and we rode to the house of Mr. Clay, the master brickmaker. We were both angry and wanted to make it there fast, so we rode very hard. When we arrived, Joe jumped down and knocked at the door. Mr. Clay came out, and Joe told him the story.

"Thank you, young man, for telling me," said Mr. Clay. "If I should bring the man before a magistrate to be judged, will you tell him what you have seen?"

"I will," answered Joe.

Mr. Clay went off to the scene, and we rode home. Joe told John all about the event, and John was very pleased.

"You did right, my boy," he said. "It is everybody's business to interfere when they see cruelty."

Later that day, Joe was called to the master's house. There was a man there who was being brought up on charges for treating horses badly. Joe was needed to give evidence. Joe brightened when he heard this.

"They will get my testimony," he

exclaimed, as he looked at me. "We won't allow such cruelty, will we, old fellow?"

We heard afterwards that the man would have to go on trial and would probably serve several months in prison. A change came over Joe. Although he was just as kind and gentle as before, he now walked tall with determination.

Chapter 13
Leaving Home

I had lived in my happy home for three years when sad news came to us all. Our mistress was still so ill that she would have to leave her home for a warmer country for awhile. The master was making plans to break us all up and leave England.

So, Merrylegs was given to the minister, who promised never to sell him. Ginger and I were sold to an earl, a friend of the master's. Joe was to take care of Merrylegs, but for some reason John was not accepting any offers.

The evening before the Squire was to leave with his wife, he came out to the stable to give his horses one last pat. He seemed very sad to me. I knew it by his voice when he spoke to John.

"Have you decided what to do, John?" he asked. "You haven't accepted any offers, have you?"

"No, sir," John answered. "I have decided to find a place with a colt breaker. I think it would be the right thing for me. Too many animals are frightened by wrong treatment. If I could help them get a fair start, I would feel that I was doing some good."

"You would be the best man I know for that job, John," the master said. "I will do all I can to help you find a place."

I certainly agreed with that. If John could have understood me, I would have told him.

The next day was very sad. Ginger and I brought the carriage to the master's door for the last time. He came down with the mistress, and they said good-bye

again to everyone. We left, then, with John driving and Joe sitting up top.

When we reached the train station, Ginger and I stood by with Joe, as John went with the master and mistress to the platform at the station. The train soon came puffing into sight and took the master and mistress away. Then we drove slowly back to Birtwick Park, a place that was no longer our happy home.

Part

2

Chapter 14

On to Earlshall

The next day was also a very sad one. The minister's wife came for Merrylegs, and John hitched Ginger and me to the carriage for our ride across the country. That day, we had to say good-bye to everyone we had lived with so happily.

We rode about fifteen miles to a place called Earlshall Park, where the earl lived. When we arrived, John asked for Mr. York. This man would be our new coachman. He was very friendly to John, but his voice told us that he expected to be obeyed.

Mr. York asked John to tell him all about us. He thought we looked well, but said that horses are just as different from one another as men are.

"Well," replied John, "I don't know of a better pair of horses. I am very unhappy to part with them. The black one has a perfect temper and has never had bad treatment. The mare, however, must have been badly treated before she came to us, because she used to kick and bite. In the last three years, she has been treated well and has behaved well, but she is more easily irritated than the black horse."

"That is good to know," said Mr. York.

"One other thing you must know," said John, "is that these horses are not used to being reined tightly. They have not worn checkreins at Birtwick. The master believed it was bad for the horses."

"I quite agree with that, but the mistress here wants the horses reined tightly," Mr. York said. "She likes for her horses to hold their heads high. It is fashionable."

"I am sorry to hear that," said John.

I had heard many bad things about checkreins. They were made to be shortened, or tightened. The shorter they became, the more the bit cut into a horse's mouth. The only way for the horse to avoid the bit was to lift his head.

John came and patted Ginger and me. He was saying good-bye. I held my head close to John, to let him know how I felt about him. Then he set off on his journey back to Birtwick, and I never saw him again.

Chapter

15

A Strike for Liberty

The next day, the earl came to look at us. He was very pleased with our appearance. York told him what John had said about us.

"Well, from what my friend Mr. Gordon has told me," he said, "both of these horses have a very fine character. They will do very well in the carriage, I think. Pay close attention to the mare and tighten the checkrein only slightly at first. They will get used to it by degrees."

Ginger and I were hitched to the

carriage that afternoon. We had to wear the checkrein, but it didn't seem too tight. We were led around to the front of the house, which was very large and very fancy. Two footmen were standing there with red breeches and white stockings.

Soon we heard silk rustling. The mistress had come down the flight of stone steps. She came around to look at us and seemed displeased, but she said nothing and got into the carriage.

The next day, we were again taken to her door. This time she came down the steps and spoke harshly to Mr. York.

"York, you must put those horses' heads higher. They look terrible."

"I beg your pardon, my lady," York replied, "but these horses have not been reined up for three years. My lord said it would be safer to get them used to it a little at a time. If your ladyship wishes, I can take them up a little more."

"Do so," she said.

That day we had a steep hill to climb. I began to understand why a checkrein is so bad. I could not pull the carriage with all my strength because I could not lower my head. If I tried, the bit cut into my mouth.

Day by day our reins were shortened. Instead of looking forward to wearing my harness and pulling the carriage, I dreaded it. Now I could better see how Ginger's temper had been spoiled.

I thought the reins couldn't possibly go any shorter. Then, one day our mistress came down the steps and ordered Mr. York to get our heads all the way up. He got down from the carriage and came around to me. The rein was shortened to much that I thought I could not possibly bear it.

Then he went over to Ginger, but she knew what was coming. As soon as Mr. York took the rein off of her to shorten it, she reared up. She hit his nose and knocked off his hat, then continued to rear and kick. I was let loose and taken from the carriage to the stables, but not before being kicked. Later, Ginger was led in by two grooms. We were both bruised.

When the earl found out about the incident, he was very upset. He decided not to have Ginger put on the carriage again. One of his younger sons thought she would make a good hunting horse, so Ginger was given to him to ride.

I began pulling the carriage with a black horse named Max, who was used to the checkrein. He told me that the checkrein would surely shorten our lives.

It just made our work too difficult to bear. It was true. Every day, we came home feeling worn out, and no one did anything to relieve us of it. Unlike at Birtwick, I felt that I didn't have one friend among the people.

Chapter

16

The Lady Anne

Early in the spring, the earl and part of his family went up to London. They took Mr. York with them and put the head groom in charge. Ginger and I, along with some other horses, were left at home.

One of the earl's daughters, Lady Anne, who remained at Earlshall Park, loved riding horseback with her brother or cousins. She was a very good rider and was certainly gentle and kind. She chose me for her horse and named me "Black Auster."

I enjoyed these rides very much. Sometimes Ginger came along. Other times Lizzie, a bright bay mare, rode with us. Lizzie was a great favorite among the men, who claimed she had a lively spirit. Ginger told me, however, that Lizzie was a nervous horse that was easily frightened.

A gentleman called Colonel Blantyre, who was staying at Earlshall park, loved to ride Lizzie. He talked of her so much that Lady Anne decided one day that she would ride her and Blantyre would take me. Blantyre tried to change her mind, but Lady Anne was determined to see how Lizzie rode.

We then set off for the village, having a message to deliver to the doctor there. When we came to the doctor's gate, Lady Anne decided she would wait on her horse and let Blantyre take the message in.

"I will be back quickly," Blantyre said, as he hung my rein on the gate.

We were standing quietly, waiting for Blantyre's return, when some cart horses and several young colts came trotting up. There was a young boy walking along behind the colts, cracking a whip. One of the colts bolted across the road and hit Lizzie. She gave a violent kick and dashed off into a gallop.

Blantyre came running out of the house when he heard me neighing. He jumped on my back, and I took off before he even had time to tell me to do so. We lost sight of Lady Anne and Lizzie

several times. Fortunately, we were told of the direction they had taken by people who had seen the young lady on the runaway horse.

Finally, we caught sight of them on the common, a place of uneven ground covered with bushes. Lizzie was headed toward a ditch. Surely, I thought, this would stop her from running. Much to my surprise, however, she took the leap. When she landed, she stumbled and fell. I took off for the ditch.

"Now, Auster, do your best," cried Blantyre.

I jumped the ditch and cleared it. Blantyre jumped off and went quickly to the mistress. She was lying face down, not moving or making a sound. Blantyre called to her but she wouldn't speak.

There were two men working on the common who were now at Blantyre's side. Blantyre asked one of them to ride and get the doctor, then to go on to Earlshall Hall and tell everyone what had happened.

So, he and I headed off on a long hard run. After alerting the doctor, we went on to Earlshall Hall. There was a great deal of excitement after we delivered the news. My bridle and saddle were taken off and a cloth was thrown over me. Ginger was then saddled up, and I soon heard the carriage roll out of the yard.

When Ginger returned, she knew only that Lady Anne was alive. It was another two days before we heard that the young mistress was out of all danger. That day, Blantyre came into the stable and patted me kindly. He said, "Black Auster, Lady Anne should never ride another horse but you." This statement made me look forward to a happy life.

Chapter

17

My Fall

Unfortunately, I would not have a happy life with Lady Anne as my friend. About one month before the family was to return from London, I had an accident. Colonel Blantyre had to return to his post in the military, so the head groom, Reuben Smith, hitched me to a carriage and drove the colonel into town.

Reuben Smith was a good man when he was sober, but every so often he fell into drinking alcohol. The master had found out and let him go. Then, later, he decided to give Reuben another chance.

That day in town, after dropping off Colonel Blantyre, Reuben went to a place called the White Lion. I was left with a hostler, a man who takes care of horses. This man noticed that a nail in one of my shoes was loose. He mentioned this when Reuben returned later that evening but Reuben told him to leave it be.

Reuben was very rough with the hostler. I could tell that he was not himself. He rode me hard, striking me with his whip and giving no thought to the loose nail.

The roads were stony, so going over them at such a fast pace caused my shoe to become looser. Finally, it came completely off, and my foot was greatly injured on the stones. I stumbled and fell on both my knees, and Reuben was flung off. When I recovered, I got to my feet and hobbled to the side of the road. Reuben lay still. He moaned a few times, but he never again moved.

Sometime later, a couple of men from Earlshall Park came along. After

examining Reuben, they said that he was dead. Seeing how badly I was injured and that my shoe was missing, they realized that Reuben had probably been drinking again. Later, after the authorities questioned the landlord and hostler at the White Lion, I was cleared of all blame.

Chapter

18

Sold

After the vet came to treat my wounds, I was put out in the pasture so I could rest. It took a long time for my knees to heal, and when the earl returned from London he was very displeased. He said that I would have to be sold.

"It is a pity," he said, "but I cannot have knees like these in my stables."

Mr. York found me a new owner in Bath. The man was a friend who owned some livery stables. He kept a number of different carriages and horses for hire. So,

I was now a "job horse," let out to all sorts of people who wished to hire me.

I found that there were many kinds of drivers. Some held the reins tightly, thinking they couldn't give a horse even a bit of freedom. Others held the reins loosely, never paying attention to what the horse was doing and never giving directions until it was too late.

One of the loose-rein types took me out one day on a country road that was being mended. Where the road was still untouched by the workmen, there were many loose stones laying about. My driver had his wife and two children with him and paid more attention to them than to his horse. So, it wasn't long before I had picked up a stone between my foot and my shoe.

My driver didn't notice that I was in pain, until much later. When he did see that I was limping, he thought that he had been given a lame horse by my master. Soon, however, a farmer came along and pointed out to him that I

probably had a stone in my shoe. The kind farmer picked up my foot, pried the stone out, and held it up.

"You see," he said. "Your horse has picked up a stone."

"That is strange," my driver replied. "I never knew that horses picked up stones."

"Well, they do!" cried the farmer, being greatly annoyed by the man's ignorance. "They can't help it on roads like these."

This was the sort of experience we job horses often had. Many times, though, there wasn't a kind farmer around to set our drivers straight.

Chapter 19
Sold Again

Sometimes we job horses met up with good drivers. I remember one morning I was put into a little gig and taken to a house. Two gentlemen came out. The taller of the two came around and looked at my bit and bridle. He shifted the collar to see if it fit comfortably.

"Please loosen the rein," he said to the livery man. He then turned to me and patted my neck. "It is a good thing not to have your mouth too bothered by that nasty bit, isn't it, old fellow?"

Then he took the reins, and both gentlemen got up into the carriage. I can remember how gently he turned me. We were soon off, and I was going at my best pace. I felt I had a driver who knew what he was doing.

This gentleman took a liking to me. After trying me several times with the saddle, he asked my master to sell me to a friend of his who wanted a safe horse for riding. In the summer, I was sold to this friend.

My new master, Mr. Barry, was also a kind man, but he had a bad time with the grooms he chose to hire. The first man turned out to be a thief. He stole all the good oats my master had ordered for me. Before Mr. Barry found out about it, I became very sick.

The next groom he hired, named Alfred Smirk, was not a groom at all. He didn't know how to properly care for horses. Because Mr. Barry knew so little, this man got away with many things.

Mr, Smirk never cleaned my shoes, but just oiled my hooves to give me the appearance of being cared for. He also left my bit rusty and my saddle damp, and he never thoroughly cleaned my stall. One day my master asked him about the bad condition of the stable.

"Alfred, shouldn't you give the stable a good cleaning?" he asked.

"Well, sir. Getting the stable wet may cause the horse to take cold, but if you wish, I will wash it out," Alfred smartly replied.

"No, then," said my master. "I would not want to cause the horse any harm."

One day my feet were so tender that, trotting over some fresh stones with my master, I made two serious stumbles. He decided as he came into the city to have my feet looked at by a farrier, a man who puts shoes on horses.

"Your horse has got the 'thrush' and badly, too," said the farrier. "This is the sort of thing we find in foul stables, where the litter is never properly cleared out.

Send your horse here tomorrow, and I will care for him."

My master was so disgusted at being deceived by two grooms that he decided to give me up after I was well. I was kept until my feet healed. Then I was sold again.

Part

3

Chapter

20

A Horse Fair

A horse fair may be a lot of fun for people, but for a horse it is not an amusing place. There is much going on, with all kinds of horses and ponies about. Some are splendid young animals that have never been badly used. Then, there are others who are sadly broken down.

Much bargaining goes on at a horse fair. Everyone wants to get a good deal. The buyers look very closely at the horses. They open a horse's mouth, look into his eyes, then feel all the way down his legs. Most of the buyers turned away

from me when they saw my badly scarred knees.

There was one man who was very gentle with me when he looked me over. I thought I would be very happy if he bought me. He offered a price but was told it was too low. He walked off, and I was very sad to see him go.

Another man walked up. He was rough with me. He, too, made an offer, the same as the nice fellow before him. By this time my salesman was thinking he would not get all the money he asked for. He was about to agree to the price when the nice fellow came back and offered more. Happily, I was his.

The money was paid, and my new master took my halter and led me to where he had a saddle and bridle ready. He gave me some good oats and stood by while I ate. Soon we were on our way to London.

We rode through the city streets, which were lit by gas lamps, and passed many houses. I thought we would never get to my new home. At last, in passing through one street, we came to a long cabstand. My rider called out in a happy voice to a driver there.

"Hello!" returned the voice. "Have you got a good one?"

"I think so," replied my owner.

We soon pulled up to a house, and my owner whistled. The door flew open,

and a young woman came out, followed
by a little girl and boy.

"Now, Harry, open the gates, and
Mother will bring us the lantern," said
my rider.

In another minute we were in the
stable, and they were all standing
around me.

"Is he gentle, Father?" asked the
young girl.

"Yes, Dolly. He's as gentle as your
kitten," he answered.

"Let me give him a bran mash while
you rub him down," said the woman.

"Do, Polly. It's just what he wants," said the man. "He's a good horse and deserves fair treatment. What do you say we call him 'Jack,' after the old one?"

"Let's do," said Polly. "I love to keep a good name going."

I was led into a clean, comfortable stall with plenty of straw. After a good supper, I rested happily. For the first time in a long while, I had found a very nice home, full of love and kindness.

Chapter

21

Jerry Barker

It was true that I had found a good home. There was never a better man than my master Jerry Barker, the cab driver. He was so good-tempered and happy that very few people could pick a fight with him. Also, he got along well with his family, and they all loved him a great deal.

Jerry's son, Harry, was clever and always did what he could to help his father. Jerry's wife, Polly, and his young daughter, Dolly, used to come into the stable in the morning and clean the cushions and the windows in the cab.

During their mornng chores, they all laughed and had a lot of fun. It was so much better to hear kind words than harsh ones. It always put me in good spirits. I felt ready each morning to go to work.

Although Jerry believed in earning a living honestly, by putting in a day's work, he never drove me hard. He wouldn't "put on the steam," he said, and wear out his poor horse just because some passenger was running late. Although, sometimes he made exceptions, if the passenger had a good reason.

Jerry had certain rules to live by. One of these was not to work on Sundays. He had learned that all people and animals needed a day of rest. He very much wanted to spend time with his wife and children, so on Sundays he did not work. For this reason, he had a six-day license for driving his cab, not a seven-day license.

One day, a man named Mr. Briggs, who was very well dressed, came into our yard to speak to Jerry. He explained

that he and his wife were now going to a different church, one that was much further away. He wanted to know if he could hire Jerry to take them to service every Sunday in the cab.

Jerry refused kindly. He told Mr. Briggs about his license and how he needed Sunday to rest and be with his family. The man reminded my master what very good customers he and his wife were, trying to change Jerry's mind. My master stood firm. He would not give up his day of rest with his family.

The man walked off angrily. Jerry was sorry to think he had lost a good customer. When he told Polly, however, she was glad that he had not given in.

During the next three weeks, Mr. and Mrs. Briggs did not call for Jerry, and he took it to heart. Now he depended more on taking work from the cabstand. There, he had to wait on strangers who wanted to go to the train station or to some other place in a great hurry.

Polly always tried to cheer him up. She said, "Just do your best, and it will all work out."

Some of the men at the cabstand, however, thought Jerry had been foolish. He had lost his best customer and now had to work harder. Some cabmen stood up for him. They said that all people and animals deserve rest.

Chapter

22

Helping Another

As it turned out, several weeks after Jerry stood his ground, Mrs. Briggs called for him to take her out. We got the news one evening from Polly. We were just getting home one evening, when she came running out with the lantern.

"It has all come right, Jerry. Mrs. Briggs sent her servant this afternoon to ask you to take her out tomorrow at eleven o'clock. I told the servant that we thought Mrs. Briggs had begun to employ another driver. The servant said

that Mr. Briggs had been put out by your refusal to work on Sunday. So, he tried other cabs, but Mrs. Briggs wasn't satisfied with any of them."

"Well, you were right, my dear," said Jerry. "I did my best, and it worked out."

After this, Mrs. Briggs wanted Jerry's cab quite often, but he was never asked to work on Sunday. However, we did have to work on one Sunday. It was an occasion when a friend needed Jerry's help.

A neighbor's mother, who lived out in the country some ten miles away, had become very sick. The neighbor, named Dinah Brown, could take a train but would still have to walk a long way to her mother's home. She herself was not strong, for she had just had a baby.

Although Jerry and I were both upset to lose our Sunday of rest, we were soon pleased to have taken the trip. Luckily, we were able to borrow the butcher's buggy, which was very light and easy for me to pull. So, the going was not so hard.

As soon as we were out in the country, where the air was sweet with the smell of fresh grass, I began to feel strong and rested. Then when we arrived at the farmhouse where Dinah's family lived, I was put into a meadow. I ate grass, rolled over on my back, and rested. Then I galloped and played. Jerry, too, had a rest. He then went down by a little brook and picked flowers.

In the afternoon we headed home

but traveled at a nice pace. When we arrived, Jerry told Polly of our time in the country. He had a restful Sunday after all and had helped another person. Polly smiled, and he handed her the flowers he had picked. Her eyes then danced with joy to see such a pretty gift.

Chapter

23

A Kind Customer

The winter came early with a great deal of wet weather. There was snow, sleet, or rain almost every day for weeks. The horses all felt it very much. When it rains, our thick blankets, which usually keep us warm in winter, get wet and do little to keep us from getting chilled.

It was really bad for us horses when the streets were slippery with frost or snow. Not being able to get a firm footing makes pulling the cabs very hard work. Also, there is the fear of falling, because it is difficult for us to keep our balance on slippery roads. When the weather was bad, Jerry sometimes went to a coffee shop for a while. When the weather was not so bad, Dolly would bring him something from home. She would run up happily to her father with a basket. Usually, Jerry had something good to eat, such as hot soup or pudding that Polly had made.

One day, when Polly had brought Jerry some soup, a young gentleman approached the cab and waved his

umbrella. Jerry started to close up his lunch and jump in the cab, but the man suddenly cried out.

"No, no, finish your soup," he said. "I am in a hurry, but I can wait until you are done."

"There, Polly," said Jerry, "is a gentleman. He shows consideration."

This man began to come to us often. I think he was very fond of animals. Whenever we took him to his home, he was met by two or three dogs. Sometimes he came around and patted me.

"This horse has got a good master," he would say, "and he deserves it." He had a pleasant voice, one that a horse could trust.

One day he and another gentleman took our cab, and we drove them to a shop. While his friend went in, our kind gentleman stood at the door. Meanwhile, across the street, a cart with two very fine horses was parked at the curb. The carter was not with them, and after awhile they began to move forward. They seemed to think it was time to leave.

The carter came out of the shop and began to scream at them and whip them. Our gentleman stepped forward quickly. He spoke to the man with a firm voice.

"If you don't stop that now," he said, "I'll have you arrested for leaving your horses and for treating them badly."

The man got into his cart and talked roughly to the gentleman. Our friend took out a notebook from his pocket and wrote down the name and address painted on the cart.

"What are you doing?" cried the carter, who was cracking his whip trying to get his horses to move on.

Our friend did not reply. He just smiled and returned to our cab. His friend had come out of the shop and had seen what had occurred.

"I would think," said the man, "that you are already too occupied with your own business to trouble yourself about other people's horses."

"The world could be a better place

for horses and people," said our friend, "if we all troubled ourselves to stop cruelty. If we see such a thing and do nothing to stop it, then we share the crime."

"I wish there were more gentlemen like you, sir," said Jerry, "for they are badly needed in this world."

Chapter

24

My Poor Old Friend

One day, while our cab and many others were waiting outside one of the parks, where a band was playing, a shabby old cab drove up. The horse was an old worn-out chestnut mare whose bones showed through her coat. There was a hopeless look in her dull eyes, and I felt sorry for her.

Suddenly, I began to think that I recognized this horse. I tried to think of where I had seen her before. She saw

me looking and then returned my gaze.

"Black Beauty, is that you?" she asked.

"Ginger? Can it be?" I returned.

"Yes, it's me," she cried.

Poor Ginger! She was so changed. Her neck was once beautifully arched and glossy. Now it was thin and fallen in. Her legs were once straight and strong, but they were now thin. Her face was once full of spirit and life, but now it was full of suffering. She was worn out from work, and I could tell that she was having a hard time breathing.

Our drivers were standing close, so I made a few steps in her direction. I asked her how her life had been since we last saw each other at Earlshall. So she told me her tale.

Ridden very hard as a hunting horse, she had become tired and short of breath. The master put her in the meadow and gave her twelve months to recover. When she was well, he sold her. Her health held up for a while, but after a long gallop one day, the old strain

returned. In this way, she was sold again and again, each time landing in a tougher spot than before.

"And so at last," she said, "I was bought by a man who owns a number of cabs and horses. He leases them to drivers, who whip me and overwork me so that they can pay the owner and still make money for themselves. I never get one day of rest."

"You used to stand up for yourself," I said. "Do you not still kick and bite when you are treated badly?"

"It's no use," she said. "I am worn down, and they are stronger than I am. If people are uncaring and cruel, there's little that animals can do to defend themselves. I wish the end would come for me. I am tired of suffering."

It made me sad to hear her talk this way. I put my nose up to hers, but I could say nothing to comfort her.

"Black Beauty," she said, "you are the only friend I ever had."

Just then her driver took on a

passenger. He pulled the reins, and Ginger had no choice but to leave. I watched her go and felt very sad, knowing her life was hard and that we would probably never see each other again.

Not many days after this, I saw a cart carrying a chestnut mare. The poor animal was thin and sunken in, and it was not breathing. I felt sure that this was Ginger, and for days afterward I felt only sorrow. She had had such a hard life.

Chapter

25

The Butcher

By this time I had seen a great deal of trouble among the horses in London. Much of this trouble might have been prevented by common sense and a kind heart. It made me very sad to see ponies straining along with heavy loads and being whipped by some cruel boy.

Once I saw a little gray pony with a thick mane and a pretty head. He was so much like Merrylegs that if I had not been in the harness I would have called to him. He was doing his best to pull a heavy cart, but a young rough boy was

cutting him under the belly with a whip. Even if it wasn't Merrylegs, I'm sure this pony was as good a fellow. He didn't deserve such treatment.

Butchers' horses were also treated badly. They were driven at great speeds through the city streets. I never knew why. Then, one day when we were waiting for our passenger, who had gone into a shop next door to a butcher's, I found out.

As we were standing there waiting, the butcher's cart came dashing up at a great pace. The horse was hot and tired. He hung his head down, while his sides heaved and his legs trembled.

The young driver jumped out of the cart and was getting his basket when the master came out looking displeased.

After examining the horse, he turned angrily to the boy.

"How many times have I told you not to drive this way?" he yelled. "You'll ruin this horse like you ruined the last. If you were not my son I would fire you. As it is, the police will probably get you for your fast driving. If that happens, don't come to me for help!"

"It is not my fault," the boy replied. "You are always saying, 'Be quick. Look sharp,' and the customers are always waiting until the very last minute to order their meat for dinner. It's nothing but hurry, hurry, all the time."

"That is all true," agreed the butcher. "No one ever thinks of a butcher's horse. You alone are not to blame. Well, just take the poor animal into the stable and look after him. If anything else is wanted from us today, you will have to carry it in your basket."

I saw things like this all the time, but I also saw kind young men who were very fond of their pony or donkey. The

animals, being patted and talked to kindly, worked cheerfully and willingly.

There was one young boy who came up our street all the time selling fruit and vegetables. He had an old pony who was full of spirit, and the two of them were the best of friends. The boy never whipped the pony, and his animal friend was always ready to work. Jerry liked the boy and said he would make a fine driver some day.

Chapter
26
A Stranger Needs Help

There came a very odd time, when something called an election was taking place. People were very rude to one another during this period, often getting into fights. When they wanted a cab, which was often, they usually wanted to get somewhere fast. We had a lot of business during the election, but the streets were very crowded and dangerous.

One day, well before the election was over, Jerry and I were taking a rest at the cabstand when a young woman with a small child walked up to us. She was looking this way and that, not knowing where she was headed. She asked Jerry if he knew the way to St. Thomas' Hospital. She had come from the country that morning in a market cart. Now, she had to carry her sick child to the hospital.

"Why, I'll take you there," said Jerry.

"Oh, no," she said. "I cannot let you do that. I have only enough money to get back home."

"But you can't get there on foot in this traffic," he cried. "Your child is heavy."

"He is, but I am strong," the mother said. "Just tell me the way, please. I can make it."

"Look here, miss," said Jerry. "I've got a wife and two dear children at home, and I know a father's feelings. Now get into the cab, and I'll take you there for nothing."

"Thank you, dear sir," she said, as she began to cry.

"Now cheer up. We'll be there soon.

Come and let me put you in the cab," he said, trying to comfort the tired woman.

Just then two men came and jumped in the cab. They were involved in the election. Jerry told them the lady was before them and that they should get out of the cab.

"Lady!" one of them cried. "She can wait. Our business is very important. Besides, we were in first and shall stay in!"

"Very well," answered Jerry. "I can wait while you have a rest."

He closed the door to the cab and turned away from them. When they understood that he would not carry them, they got out. We were on our way to the hospital within a few minutes, after listening to their angry shouts and threats to call the police.

When we got to the hospital, Jerry helped the woman take her child in. He returned not long after that and was getting ready to pull away from the curb when someone called his name. Jerry seemed to know her at once.

"Jeremiah Barker!" she cried. "I am so glad to see you. It is so difficult to get a cab in London these days."

"I shall be proud to serve you, ma'am. I am glad I happened to be here. Where may I take you, ma'am?"

"To the Paddington Station, and then if we have some time I would like for you to tell me about Polly and the children."

We got to the station early enough for Jerry and the lady to have a talk. I

found out that she had been Polly's employer. Before she got on her train, she told Jerry that if he ever wanted to give up driving a cab he should let her know.

With that she handed him some money for the cab ride and a great deal more for the children. Jerry thanked her, and we headed home. I could tell he was pleased to have seen this lady. She seemed to me like a very kind woman.

Chapter 27

Jerry's New Year

Christmas and the New Year are very merry times for some people, but for cabmen and cabmen's horses it is no holiday. There are so many parties and dances for people to go to, that there is much work for the cabs. Often, drivers and their horses stand in the rain or frost, shivering with cold as they wait for their customers. Then, it is very late when they get home.

During the Christmas week, Jerry and I worked late every night. Polly sat

up waiting for us. She always came out
with the lantern as soon as we rolled in.

It was very cold during that time,
and Jerry began to cough and look ill.
Polly always looked troubled when she
came out to meet us. She helped put me
in the stable and then got Jerry something warm to eat.

On New Year's Eve, we had to take
two gentlemen to a house. We left them at
nine o'clock and were supposed to return
at eleven. We returned on time, but no
one came out the door, so we waited.

The weather was very bad that night. It had rained all day, and now the wind drove the sleet against us. Jerry got down and came to me, pulling my blanket closer around my neck. He then started to move about, trying to keep himself warm. Soon he was coughing violently.

At some point after midnight, Jerry
went up to the door of the house and
rang the bell. He asked the servant if
anyone would be wanting his services
that night. The servant answered yes, so

Jerry went back to the cab and continued to wait.

It was another hour before the two gentlemen came out. They got in without giving an apology. When they found out that they were being charged for the time we waited, they said they were sorry. But they were really angry. They thought Jerry was overcharging them. He stood his ground, and they paid us.

Jerry's cough had grown much worse. By the time we got home he could hardly speak. Polly met us with the

lamp and asked if she could do something to help him.

"Yes, please," he answered with a whisper of a voice. "Give our horse Jack something warm, and then make something for me as well."

After Jerry gave me a rubdown and threw down some hay, he headed into the house. I, too, was tired and cold. After a warm meal, I quickly fell asleep.

Chapter

28

Sad News For Me

The next morning, little Harry came out to clean my stall and feed me. Jerry never came down, so I didn't work that day at all. Then, another two days passed without seeing Jerry.

Finally, when Harry came to feed me one morning, a cabman by the name of Governor Grant came into the stable and asked about Jerry. Harry said that he was very ill. He had something called bronchitis. The cabman looked very upset and said that an illness such as that was very serious.

For a week or more, Harry came down to feed me and clean my stall. Jerry was getting better, but the doctor told him that he should never go back to cab work again. Harry and Dolly talked about what would happen if their father could not go back to work. They were very worried, it seemed to me.

One day young Dolly came down while Harry was in my stall. She was very excited and seemed full of news.

"Who lives at Fairstowe?" she asked. "Mother has got a letter from there. She seemed very glad. She ran upstairs to Father with it."

"Don't you know? Why, it is the name of Mrs. Fowler's place—mother's old mistress, you know—the lady that father met last summer. He took her to the train station, and she gave him money."

Dolly went back in the house, but in a few minutes she was back in the stable.

"Oh! Harry, there was never anything so wonderful. Mrs. Fowler says we are to go live near her. There is a cottage

for us there, with a garden and a hen-house, and apple trees! She will want father for a coachman in the spring."

"That's just the right thing for us all!" said Harry. "I'll be a groom, too, or a gardener."

Soon it was decided that Jerry and his family would leave the city. I would be sold, along with the cab. This was very sad news to me. Since leaving Birtwick, I had never been so happy as with my dear master Jerry. I was sure he would try to find me a good home, but I knew that no place could be an improvement on the home I was now losing.

Part

4

Chapter 29

Hard Times

I was sold to a baker, with whom Jerry thought I would have good food and fair work. If my new master had always been present, I think things would have gone well. As it happened, I was often overloaded.

There was a foreman there who was always hurrying everyone. Usually, when I already had a full load, he would order my carter to pile on more. My carter tried to reason with the man but was always overruled.

This job wore me down in a very short time. I had to pull heavy loads up steep hills all day. When I slowed down, I was whipped. Finally, a younger horse was brought in, and I was being sold off. My new master, who owned a cab company, cared only for his money. He spoke to his drivers in a rough manner,

with a voice as harsh as the grinding of cart wheels over gravel. They in turn were rough with the horses.

It was with this company that I learned how really hard a cab horse's life could be. I had no day of rest, and I was fed only at night. My driver whipped me constantly, sometimes under the belly. This treatment took the spirit out of me, and soon I wished to be put out of my misery.

One day, after having taken a passenger to the train station, my driver pulled up behind some other cabs, hoping to get another passenger. After a short wait, a family came up to our cab. They had a lot of luggage, and the porter suggested to the man that he hire two cabs. The man asked my driver if I would be able to handle the load, and my driver assured him I would. The man's little girl came over to me and looked into my eyes. She turned back to her father then.

"Papa," she said, "I am sure this poor horse cannot take us and all our luggage

so far. He is so very weak and worn out."

"Nonsense, Grace," he said. "Get in the cab and don't make a fuss. I'm sure this man knows his business. If he says his horse can take us, then we will take this one cab."

Everything was loaded onto my cab, and the people climbed in. It was all so heavy that the cab sank on its springs closer to the road. The driver paid it little attention and signaled me with a great lash of the whip to pull out of the station.

I did well until we came to a hill. I tried as best I could to pull the cab up that hill, but my feet slipped. Suddenly, I fell to the ground on my side and felt the breath knocked out of me. I had no power to move. I just lay there and closed my eyes, thinking that I was at my end.

Something was poured down my throat, and a blanket was placed over me. After awhile I was able to get up, and someone led me to a stable. There, I rested for a few days.

My master was angry. The doctor

told him I would never be good for cab work again. Luckily, this doctor suggested that I be nursed for a couple of weeks and taken to a horse sale. That way my master would not lose the money he had paid for me.

So, it was decided that I would be sold once again. This time I wasn't sad or afraid to leave. I felt that nothing could be worse than a cab company.

Chapter

30

The Farmer and His Grandson

At the horse sale, I found myself in the company of old, broken-down horses and poor old men. The buyers were trying to get a horse or pony that might drag a little cart for wood or coal. The sellers were trying to get a little money for their worn-out beasts, rather than suffering the complete loss of having to kill them.

Lucky for me, a gentleman farmer came up and looked me over. He had a broad back and round shoulders and wore a wide-brimmed hat. I pricked up my ears and looked at him.

"There's a horse, Willie, that has known better days," he said.

"Poor old fellow!" said the young boy at his side. "Do you think, Grandpapa, he was ever a carriage horse?"

"Oh, yes!" said the farmer. "He might have been anything when he was young. Look at the shape of his neck and shoulders. There's a great deal of breeding there."

He patted my neck, and I put my nose against him, nudging him gently.

"See how well he understands kindness, Grandpapa?" the boy exclaimed. "Couldn't you buy him and make him young again, like you did with Ladybird?"

"Ladybird was not so old."

"Well, Grandpapa. I don't believe that this horse is so old."

The old man laughed, and the man who had brought me to the sale now started to talk.

"The young man is right. This horse is not so old. He's just run down from overwork. He just needs some rest."

The farmer slowly felt my legs then looked at my mouth. He thought for a moment, then asked the price. He could see that his grandson was excited and wanted to help me, so he pulled out his purse and counted out his money.

I, too, was excited. I felt that this man was gentle and that his grandson wanted to take care of me. They walked forward, and I was led behind. I had a good feed and was then gently ridden to my new master's home, where I was turned out into a meadow.

My master, called Mr. Thoroughgood, gave orders that I should have hay and oats every night and morning. I was also to be let loose in the meadow during the day. Young Willie was to be in charge of taking care of me.

Willie did his job well, and the care-taking began to improve my condition. During the winter my legs healed and became strong. Not being so stiff, I felt young again.

"He's growing young, Willie," said

the farmer one day in the spring. "He has good paces. They couldn't be better."

"Oh, Grandpapa, how glad I am you bought him!"

"So am I, my boy, but he has you to thank for that. We must now start looking for a gentle place for him, where he will be valued."

Chapter

31

My Last Home

One day during the summer, the groom cleaned and dressed me with such care that I thought something was about to happen. Willie seemed anxious, yet happy. They hitched me to a buggy, and we rode to a pretty house with a lawn and shrubbery at the front.

"If the ladies take to him," said the farmer, "he'll get a good home."

Willie went up to the door and rang the bell. He asked if Miss Blomefield or

Miss Ellen were at home. They were. So, while Willie stayed with me, Mr. Thoroughgood went into the house.

In a few minutes, he returned with three ladies. They all looked at me and asked questions. One looked at my knees and asked if I would fall down again. That, she said, would give her a terrible fright.

"Many horses have their knees

injured by careless drivers," answered the farmer. "From what I see of this horse, his injury was no fault of his own. If you want, you can just try him for awhile. Your coachman can see what he thinks of him."

"You have always been such a good adviser to us about our horses," said the lady, "that your recommendation means a lot. We will try him."

The next day, a young man came to Farmer Thoroughgood's place to take me to my new home. When this young man saw my knees, he looked displeased.

"I would not have thought that you would recommend such a horse to the ladies," he said.

"You are only taking him on trial," the farmer answered. "If he is not as safe as any horse you ever drove, then send him back."

I was taken home, placed in a stable, fed, and left to myself. The next day my groom came in. While he was cleaning me, he noticed my white markings.

"That is just like the star that Black Beauty had," he said aloud. "This horse is about the same height, too. I wonder where Black Beauty is now."

As he continued to brush, he noticed more things about me that seemed familiar.

"He has one white foot and that little patch of white hair in the middle of his back, the one that John used to call 'Beauty's threepenny bit.' This must be Black Beauty! Why, Beauty, do you know me? I'm Joe Green, the one who almost caused your death."

He began patting me and patting me. He was so overjoyed.

I could not say that I remembered him at once. He was all grown up now. But when I did remember him, I nudged him with my nose and neighed. I never saw a man so pleased.

"Give you a fair trial, they said! I wonder who it was that broke your knees. You must have been badly treated. Well, I'll see to it that you have a good life here, old friend."

In the afternoon, Joe told the three sisters that he was sure I was Squire Gordon's old Black Beauty. One said she would be sure to write to Mrs. Gordon and tell her. After this, I was driven every day for a week or so, and the sisters were very pleased with me. They decided to keep me and call me by my old name.

I have a real home now, for the ladies have promised that I shall never be sold. My work is pleasant, and Joe is the best and kindest of grooms. I see

Willie all the time and receive lots of friendly pats from the people who work for the sisters. My troubles are finally over. I now feel as good as I did when I was young, when I stood with my friends under the apple trees at Birtwick.

THE END

Glossary and Pronunciation Guide

advice (ad-VYS) an opinion about what to do or how to act; *p. 16*

bit (BIT) a metal bar worn in a horse's mouth to which the reins are attached. This allows a rider to steer and control the horse; *p. 21*

blinkers (BLINK-urs) rectangular pieces of leather worn on each side of a horse's head to keep the horse from seeing what is off to the side; *p. 22*

bridle (BRY-dul) the headgear worn by a horse so that a person can direct and steer it; *p, 21*

bronchitis (bron-KY-tus) a dangerous sickness of the lungs; *p. 163*

checkreins (CHEK-raynz) short reins, painful for a horse to wear, that force a horse to hold its head high; *p. 83*

colt (KOLT) a young male horse; *p. 15*

dignity (DIG-nuh-tee) feeling of self-worth; *p, 46*

evidence (EV-uh-dents) proof of something, often presented in court; *p. 73*

farrier (FAIR-ee-ur) a person who puts shoes on horses; *p. 110*

fond (FAHND) having a liking for; *p. 135*

foreman (FOR-mun) a person in charge of a group of workers; *p. 169*

foul (FOWL) dirty and disgusting; *p. 110*

gig (GIG) a small, two-wheeled carriage pulled by a horse; *p. 107*

halter (HAWL-tur) a rope or strap for leading or tying an animal, such as a horse; *p, 20*

ill-tempered (ILL TEM-purd) being in a bad mood; *p. 27*

improvement (im-PROOV-ment) an increase in quality; *p. 166*

leases (LEES-ez) rents to someone else for his or her long-term use; *p. 142*

livery stables (LIV-uh-ree STAY-bulz) a place where horses are kept and where horses and carriages can be hired for use; *p. 103*

magistrate (MAJ-is-trayt) a judge; *p. 73*

moped (MOPD) was lazy and inactive because of sadness or disappointment; *p. 64*

overcharging (oh-vur-CHARJ-ing) demanding a price that is too high; *p. 161*

plowboy (PLOW-boy) a boy who leads a team of horses pulling a plow; *p. 16*

skittish (SKIT-ish) nervous and jumpy; *p. 36*

testimony (TES-tuh-MOH-nee) a person's official account of a story or event; *p. 73*

upbringing (UP-bring-ing) way of being raised or brought up; *p. 37*

About the Author

Anna Sewell was born in 1820 in Yarmouth, England. Her parents were Quakers, and their household was very involved in social reform. Anna's mother was a best-selling author, and her father was a businessman.

As a young girl, Sewell was in an accident that left her crippled. Afterward, she had to get around the countryside on a horse or go by horse cart. This experience caused her to have a deep fondness for horses.

Sewell's story *Black Beauty* shows how much she understood and appreciated horses. The book was published only a few months before she died in 1878. She was buried in a Quaker cemetery in Boston, England.

VALUES IN ACTION™
Illustrated Classics

Series 1
The Adventures of Tom Sawyer
Black Beauty
Gulliver's Travels
Heidi
Jane Eyre
Little Women
Moby Dick
The Red Badge of Courage
Robinson Crusoe
The Secret Garden
Swiss Family Robinson
White Fang

Teacher's Guide available for each series

Series 2
The Adventures of Huckleberry Finn
The Adventures of Robin Hood
The Adventures of Sherlock Holmes
Alice in Wonderland
Call of the Wild
Frankenstein
The Hunchback of Notre Dame
A Little Princess
Oliver Twist
The Prince and the Pauper
The Strange Case of Dr. Jekyll and Mr. Hyde
Treasure Island

www.readingchallenge.com